Little Stars

Little Stars YOGA

A CRABTREE SEEDLINGS BOOK

Taylor Farley

I love **yoga**.

3

Yoga makes me feel **calm**.

I use a yoga mat.

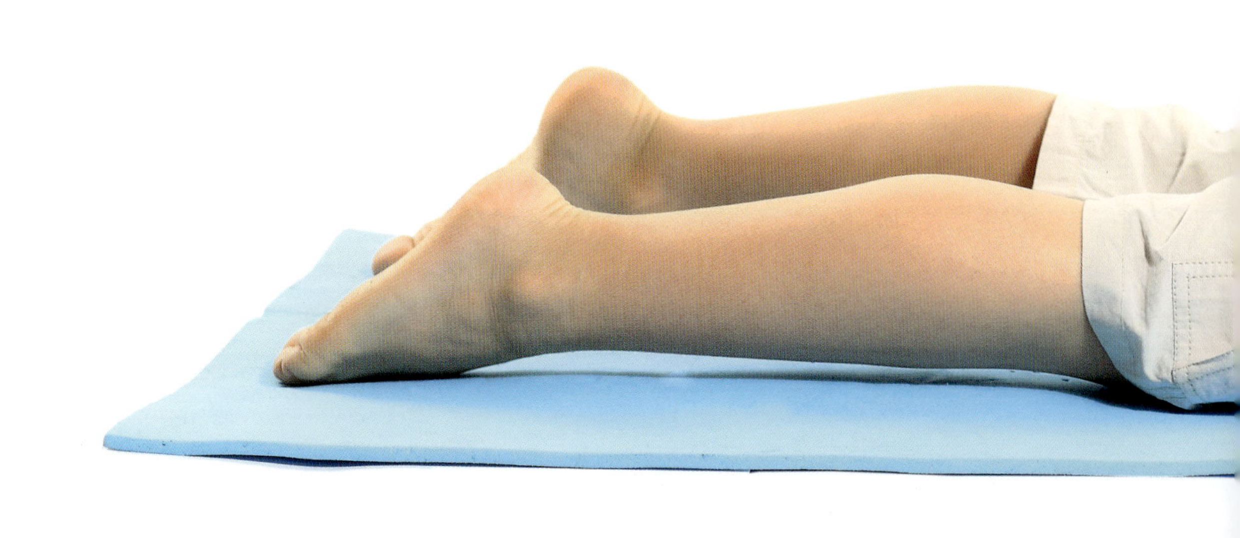

I wear **comfy** clothes.

I take deep **breaths**.

I stretch into a warrior **pose**.

I bend into camel pose.

I balance in tree pose.

Yoga makes me strong.

I **practice** yoga every day.

Glossary

breaths (BRETHS): Breaths are the air that you breathe into and out of your lungs.

calm (KAHM): When you feel calm, you feel peaceful and not worried.

comfy (KUHM-fee): Comfy means comfortable. Clothes that are comfy make you feel relaxed and able to move easily.

pose (POHZ): To pose is to position your body in a certain way.

practice (PRAK-tiss): Practice is doing something over and over for improvement.

yoga (YOH-guh): Yoga is a set of exercises for the mind and body.

Index

breaths 11
camel pose 14
clothes 8
tree pose 16
warrior pose 13
yoga mat 6

School-to-Home Support for Caregivers and Teachers

Crabtree Seedlings books help children grow by letting them practice reading. Here are a few guiding questions to help the reader build his or her comprehension skills. Possible answers are included.

Before Reading

- **What do I think this book is about?** I think this book is about yoga. It might tell us about why people like to do yoga.
- **What do I want to learn about this topic?** I want to learn about different yoga poses.

During Reading

- **I wonder why...** I wonder why the children wear comfy clothes when they do yoga.
- **What have I learned so far?** I learned about different yoga poses called warrior pose, camel pose, and tree pose.

After Reading

- **What details did I learn about this topic?** I learned that children like to do yoga because it makes them feel calm and strong.
- **Write down unfamiliar words and ask questions to help understand their meaning.** I see the word *calm* on page 5 and the word *breaths* on page 11. The other vocabulary words are listed on pages 22 and 23.

Library and Archives Canada Cataloguing in Publication

Title: Little stars yoga / Taylor Farley.
Names: Farley, Taylor, author.
Description: Series statement: Little stars | "A Crabtree seedlings book". | Includes index. |
Previously published in electronic format by Blue Door Education in 2020.
Identifiers: Canadiana 20200379836 | ISBN 9781427129901 (hardcover) | ISBN 9781427130082 (softcover)
Subjects: LCSH: Hatha yoga for children—Juvenile literature. | LCSH: Hatha yoga—Juvenile literature.
Classification: LCC RJ133.7 .F37 2021 | DDC j613.7/046083—dc23

Library of Congress Cataloging-in-Publication Data

Names: Farley, Taylor, author.
Title: Little stars yoga / Taylor Farley.
Description: New York, NY : Crabtree Publishing Company, 2021. | Series: Little stars; a Crabtree seedlings book | Includes index. |
Identifiers: LCCN 2020049331 | ISBN 9781427129901 (hardcover) | ISBN 9781427130082 (paperback)
Subjects: LCSH: Hatha yoga for children--Juvenile literature.
Classification: LCC RJ133.7 .F37 2021 | DDC 613.7/046083--dc23
LC record available at https://lccn.loc.gov/2020049331

Crabtree Publishing Company
www.crabtreebooks.com 1–800–387–7650

e-book ISBN 978-0-997240-17-7

Print book version produced jointly with Blue Door Education in 2021

Written by Taylor Farley
Production coordinator and Prepress technician: Samara Parent
Print coordinator: Katherine Berti

Printed in the U.S.A./012021/CG20201102

Photo credits: Cover and pages 3 and 21 © DoublePHOTO studio; page 4 © Duplass; pages 6 and 7 © YURALAITS ALBERT, page 9 © Rob Marmion; page 10 © Eugene Partyzan; page 12 © Max Topchii; page 15 © Nick_Nick; page 17 © Patrick Foto; page 18 © Nick_Nick
All photos from Shutterstock.com

Published in Canada
Crabtree Publishing
616 Welland Ave.
St. Catharines, Ontario
L2M 5V6

Published in the United States
Crabtree Publishing
347 Fifth Ave.
Suite 1402-145
New York, NY 10016

Published in the United Kingdom
Crabtree Publishing
Maritime House
Basin Road North, Hove
BN41 1WR

Published in Australia
Crabtree Publishing
Unit 3 – 5 Currumbin Court
Capalaba
QLD 4157